GULLIVER IN LILLIPUT

retold by Margaret Hodges
from Gulliver's Travels by
Jonathan Swift

illustrated by Kimberly Bulcken Root

Holiday House/New York

For Fletcher, my fellow traveler
M.H.

*For Jeanette M., Nancy, Marian, Mike and Janice, Don
and Sharon, Jake and Sue, Gloria, Jeanette D., Dave,
Fred, Dallas, Shelly, Norm and Linda, and Barry
—Sunday, 10:15*
K.B.R.

Text copyright © 1995 by Margaret Hodges
Illustrations copyright © 1995 by Kimberly Bulcken Root
All rights reserved
Printed in the United States of America
First Edition

Library of Congress Cataloging-in-Publication Data
Hodges, Margaret, 1911–
Gulliver in Lilliput / retold by Margaret Hodges from Gulliver's
Travels by Jonathan Swift ; illustrated by Kimberly Bulcken Root. —
1st ed.
p.   cm.
Summary: On a voyage in the South Seas, an Englishman finds
himself shipwrecked in Lilliput, a land of people only six
inches high.
ISBN 0-8234-1147-8
[1. Fantasy.   2. Size—Fiction.]   I. Root, Kimberly Bulcken, ill.
II. Swift, Jonathan, 1667–1745. Gulliver's travels.   III. Title.
PZ7.H6644Gu   1995   94-15037   CIP   AC
[Fic]—dc20

AUTHOR'S NOTE

Jonathan Swift wrote *Gulliver's Travels* for grown-up readers. He described the adventures of an Englishman, Lemuel Gulliver, who sailed to strange lands that no one else had ever seen. From strange lands sailors bring home souvenirs and strange stories which they love to tell to children as well as to grown-ups. This story, *Gulliver in Lilliput*, Part I of *Gulliver's Travels*, is told as Gulliver might have told the first of his adventures to children.

A Long Voyage and a Disaster

I grew up in the quiet English countryside and might never have left home, except that my father had five sons and not much money to educate them. So, as soon as I reached manhood, I went to work with a well-known surgeon in London, intending to be a doctor myself. At the same time I studied all the subjects useful for long voyages, because I had always wanted to travel.

For three years I did voyage to foreign countries and earned enough money to marry, but as a young doctor I had few patients and decided to go to sea again in order to support my wife and children, a boy and a girl.

On May 4, 1699, I set sail from Bristol with Captain William Prichard, captain of the *Antelope*.

Our voyage went very well until we reached the South Seas, by which time our crew were sick with overwork and bad food. Then a violent storm drove us onto a rock which split the ship in two. Six of us managed to lower a boat into the sea and rowed with what little strength we had until a sudden gust of wind overturned us, and all the others were drowned.

I swam, pushed forward by time and tide, and when I was almost exhausted, I saw land, and found myself in shallow water. At about eight o'clock in the evening, I got to the shore and walked for nearly half a mile without seeing any houses or people. Too tired to go farther, I lay down on my back in the grass, which was very short and soft. There I slept soundly until morning.

Captured

When I awakened, it was just daylight. I tried to rise, but was not able to stir, because my arms and legs were strongly fastened to the ground. So was my hair, which was long and thick. I also felt several slender cords across my body, from my armpits to my thighs. Unable to move my head, I could only look up. Meanwhile, the sun began to grow hot, and the light hurt my eyes. I heard a confused noise about me, but could see only the sky.

In a little while I felt something alive moving on my left leg, then over my chest and almost up to my chin. Looking down as much as I could, I saw a little man not six inches high with a bow and arrow in his hands and a quiver at his back. Then I felt at least forty more little men following the first. I shouted so loud that they all ran back, and afterward I was told that some of them were hurt with the falls they got by leaping from my sides to the ground. However, they soon returned, and one of them, staring at my face in admiration, cried out in a shrill, clear voice, "*Hekinah degul.*" The others repeated these words, but I did not know what they meant.

At last, struggling to get loose, I broke the strings and wrenched out the pegs that fastened my left arm to the ground. At the same time, with much pain, I pulled loose the strings that tied down my hair on the left side, so that I could turn my head about two inches. But again the little people ran off before I could catch them.

Then I heard one of them cry, "*Tolgo phonac*," and a hundred arrows struck my left hand, pricking like needles. I used my free hand to cover my face on which more arrows were falling. Some of the little people tried to stick spears into my side, but my jacket was too thick. I decided to lie still until night, when it would be easier to free myself.

Soon I heard a sound of hammering and saw the little men building a platform about a foot-and-a-half high, big enough to hold four of them. One, who looked important, climbed up on the platform and made a long speech. Even though I knew he could not understand, I answered, "Are you threatening me? Or are you promising to show pity and treat me kindly?" Then I said in a gentle voice, "Whatever you order me to do, I will obey, but I have not eaten for many hours. Please feed me." I put my finger on my mouth to show that I was hungry.

The leader understood me. He ordered ladders to be placed against my sides, after which about a hundred of the little people climbed up and walked toward my mouth, carrying baskets of food. There were several kinds of meat, as well as three loaves of bread, each no bigger than a bullet.

When I made a sign that I wanted to drink, the people hoisted up a hogshead of their wine and pushed it toward my hand. It held less than half a pint, not strong, but delicious. When I asked for more, my captors danced on my chest and shouted for joy to see such a wonder. They rubbed my face and hands with a sweet-smelling ointment that soon removed the sting of their arrows. I was tempted to seize forty or fifty of them as they walked over me, but I remembered that I had promised to obey them, and I was grateful for their hospitality. Also I admired the courage of these tiny creatures who dared to walk on my body while I had one hand free.

Another leader now came forward and told me by sign language that the emperor wished me to be carried as a prisoner to the capital city. That night, while I slept, they brought a wooden frame, seven feet long and four feet wide, mounted on twenty-two wheels, with nine hundred of their strongest men to lift me onto it. Fifteen hundred of the emperor's largest horses, each about four-and-a-half inches high, then dragged me to the city, half a mile away.

My New Home

They stopped in front of an ancient temple, the largest in the whole kingdom. There I was to live, and a hundred thousand little people came out of the town to watch me being moved into my new home. The emperor himself looked on while his blacksmith padlocked long chains to my left leg and fastened them to the gate. The chains were about six feet long so that once the strings were cut that still bound me, I could stand up and walk backward and forward and in a small semi-circle. When I did so, no words can describe the noise and astonishment of the people.

Looking around me, I saw a little country like a garden with woods among the flower beds. As I stood there, the royal family arrived and sat down at a safe distance, while the emperor rode up alone to me and began to speak. I answered in all the languages that I knew, but neither of us could understand a word.

His Majesty left guards to protect me, and when some of the crowd shot arrows at me, the guards handed over six of the ringleaders so that I could punish them. I put five of them into my coat pocket. Then, holding the sixth man in my hand, I took out my penknife as if I were going to eat him alive. But instead I set him gently on the ground and took the others, one by one, out of my pocket. Away they all ran, and I could see that the soldiers and people were pleased with my kindness.

I slept on the ground in my house for about two weeks until the emperor ordered a bed for me, made of six hundred little mattresses, sewn together and provided with sheets, blankets, and coverlets.

Meanwhile, the emperor's courtiers feared that I might break loose and eat enough to cause a famine. They thought of starving me to death or shooting me with poisoned arrows. But some army officers reported my kindness to the six criminals, and as a result, an order was given that the villages must provide my daily food and drink, including six cows, forty sheep, and bread and wine, for which the emperor would pay from his own treasury. Six hundred people were set up in tents by my door to be my servants, three hundred tailors went to work on a new suit of clothes for me, and six of His Majesty's greatest scholars began to teach me their language. I then learned that this land was called Lilliput; the people were called Lilliputians. They called me *Quinbus Flestrin*, which means Great Man Mountain.

My Pockets

The emperor came often to visit me, and each time I got down on my knees, saying, "Your Majesty, I beg you to set me free."

But he answered, "That is impossible without the consent of my council." Finally, one day, he said, "Quinbus Flestrin, I hope that before you are set free, you will not object if two of my soldiers search you for dangerous weapons."

I put the soldiers into all of my pockets and they later made a list of what they had found. They wrote:

"In the right coat pocket of the Man Mountain was a great piece of coarse cloth, large enough to be a rug in the royal palace. [This was my handkerchief.]

"In the left pocket was a huge silver chest. We asked the Man Mountain to open it, and when one of us stepped into it, he found himself up to his knees in some sort of dust that made us sneeze. [This was my snuffbox.]

"In one waistcoat pocket was a bundle of paper, [my diary], tied up with a cable and covered with black marks. In another we found a kind of machine with twenty long poles attached to it. We suppose that the Man Mountain uses it to comb his hair.

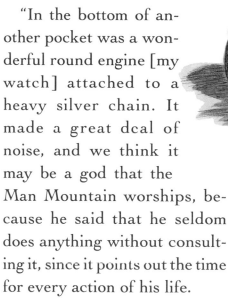

"In the right side of his breeches we saw a hollow pillar of iron as tall as a man, fastened to a strong piece of wood. In the left side of his breeches was another of the same kind. We do not know what they are. [They were my pistols.]

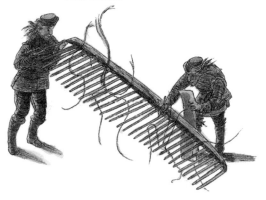

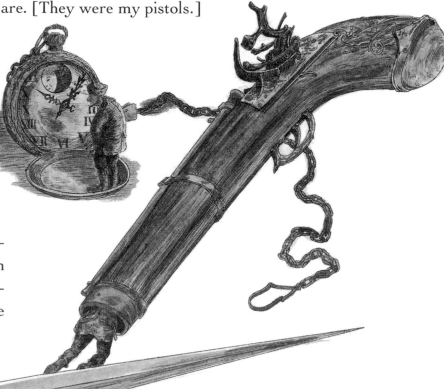

"In the bottom of another pocket was a wonderful round engine [my watch] attached to a heavy silver chain. It made a great deal of noise, and we think it may be a god that the Man Mountain worships, because he said that he seldom does anything without consulting it, since it points out the time for every action of his life.

At his side hangs a sword as long as five men. He has a bag full of some heavy metal balls [bullets] and another full of black powder [gunpowder]."

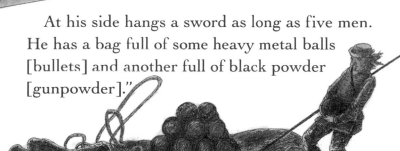

The emperor ordered me to hand over all of these things that were in my pockets, which I did, but I had one pocket that the soldiers did not find. There I carried a pair of spectacles and a pocket spyglass. Before handing over all that was in the other pockets, at the emperor's command, I waved my sword in the air and fired off my pistols to show how they worked. The pistols were charged only with gunpowder, but hundreds of Lilliputians fell down at the noise, as if they had been struck dead, and even the emperor looked frightened.

I could now understand and speak their language. I would sometimes lie down and let five or six of them dance on my hand. Boys and girls would play at hide-and-seek in my hair. The horses were no longer afraid of me and their riders would make them leap over my hand as I held it on the ground. Before long, my gentleness and good behavior pleased all the Lilliputians so much that I was set free.

Lilliput Goes to War

Soon afterward, one of the emperor's officers came to speak to me. I held him in my hand during our conversation. "The reason you won your freedom so easily," said he, "is that Lilliput has two great troubles. First, we have two political parties in this empire, the Tramecksan, who wear high heels, and the Slamecksan, who wear low heels. The two parties will not even talk to each other. His Majesty prefers low heels, and he wants your help.

"Second, we are in danger of an invasion from Blefuscu. Now, Blefuscu is the other great empire of the universe. Our history books do not mention any empires except Lilliput and Blefuscu. These two mighty powers have been at war for the past thirty-six moons. The reason is that, as we all know, the old way of breaking a boiled egg before eating was to break the big end. But when our emperor's grandfather was a boy, he cut one of his fingers while breaking an egg at the big end. The people were then ordered to break only the smaller end of their eggs. The Lilliputians who did not like this way of breaking their eggs — the Big Endians — fled to Blefuscu, which sided with them and went to war with Lilliput. Both empires have lost their finest ships and many smaller ones as well as thousands of soldiers and seamen. Our emperor has asked me to tell you that Blefuscu now has a new fleet ready to attack us."

I replied, "Please tell His Majesty that it would not be right for me to interfere with political parties, but that I am ready to risk my life if Lilliput should be invaded by Blefuscu."

The empire of Blefuscu is an island on the northeast side of Lilliput, separated by a channel that is eight hundred yards wide. When I heard of the coming invasion from Blefuscu, I kept away from that side of the coast, so that the enemy's ships could not see me, while I could see them with my pocket spyglass. Then I went to the royal palace and spoke to the emperor: "Your Majesty, I have a plan to seize the enemy's entire navy, which lies in a harbor at Blefuscu, ready to sail."

The emperor agreed to my plan, so I talked to the Lilliputian seamen. From them I learned that the middle of the channel was seventy *glumgluffs* deep, which is about six feet. With the emperor's permission, I ordered a great quantity of Lilliput's strongest cable and bars of iron. The cable was no thicker than a heavy thread, and the iron bars the size of knitting needles, so I twisted them together, three by three, to make them stronger, and did the same with the iron bars, making their ends into hooks.

I Attack Blefuscu

Having fixed fifty hooks to the cables, I went to the northeast coast about half an hour before high tide. Taking off my coat, shoes, and stockings, I then walked into the sea. I waded as fast as I could, and as I reached the deepest water, swam till I felt ground under my feet. Within half an hour, I had reached the fleet in the harbor at Blefuscu.

The enemy were so frightened when they saw me coming that they leaped out of their ships, and swam to shore, where at least thirty thousand little people were watching. I then fastened a hook to a hole in the prow of each vessel. While I was tying all the cords together into a knot at the end, the enemy shot several thousand arrows at me, stinging my hands and face and making my work more difficult. I would certainly have lost my eyesight if I had not put on the spectacles that were still in the private pocket the emperor's searchers had not found.

But when I had fastened all the hooks to the ships and had begun to pull, not a ship would stir because they were all held fast by their anchors. I had to cut the anchor cables, while more than two hundred arrows struck my face and hands. Then I again took up the knot end of the cables to which my hooks were tied, and easily drew fifty of the enemy's largest warships after me.

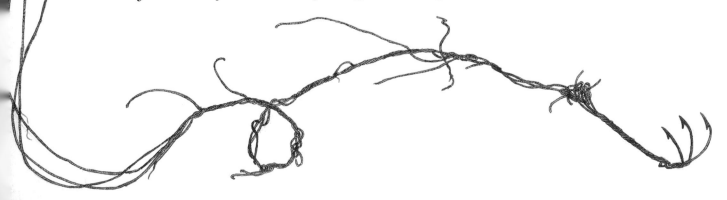

Victory!

The people of Blefuscu were stunned. They had thought at first that I only intended to let the ships drift about and crash into each other. But when they saw me pulling the whole fleet out into the channel, they gave a great scream of grief and despair. Once out of danger, I stopped a while to pick the arrows out of my hands and face and rub on some of the healing ointment given to me earlier by the Lilliputians. Then, when the tide had fallen a little, I waded through the channel with my cargo, and arrived safely at the royal port of Lilliput.

"Long live the emperor of Lilliput!" I cried. His Majesty gave me the greatest praise. "Man Mountain," he said, "I make you a *nardac*, which is the highest title of honor in Lilliput. But return to Blefuscu and capture all the rest of our enemy's ships. Defeat Blefuscu so completely that I can become its emperor, and therefore the emperor of the whole world with power to make the Big Endian exiles break the smaller end of their eggs."

"But Your Majesty," I protested, "I could never take part in destroying a free and brave people."

The emperor frowned at this, but said no more for the time being.

The emperor of Blefuscu heard of our argument and about three weeks later sent ambassadors humbly asking for a peace treaty and thanking me for my help.

They then gave me an invitation: "The emperor of Blefuscu wishes you to visit his kingdom so that he may have the pleasure of seeing you demonstrate your enormous strength of which he has heard so much."

I asked permission of the emperor of Lilliput, and he agreed to let me visit Blefuscu, but did not look pleased.

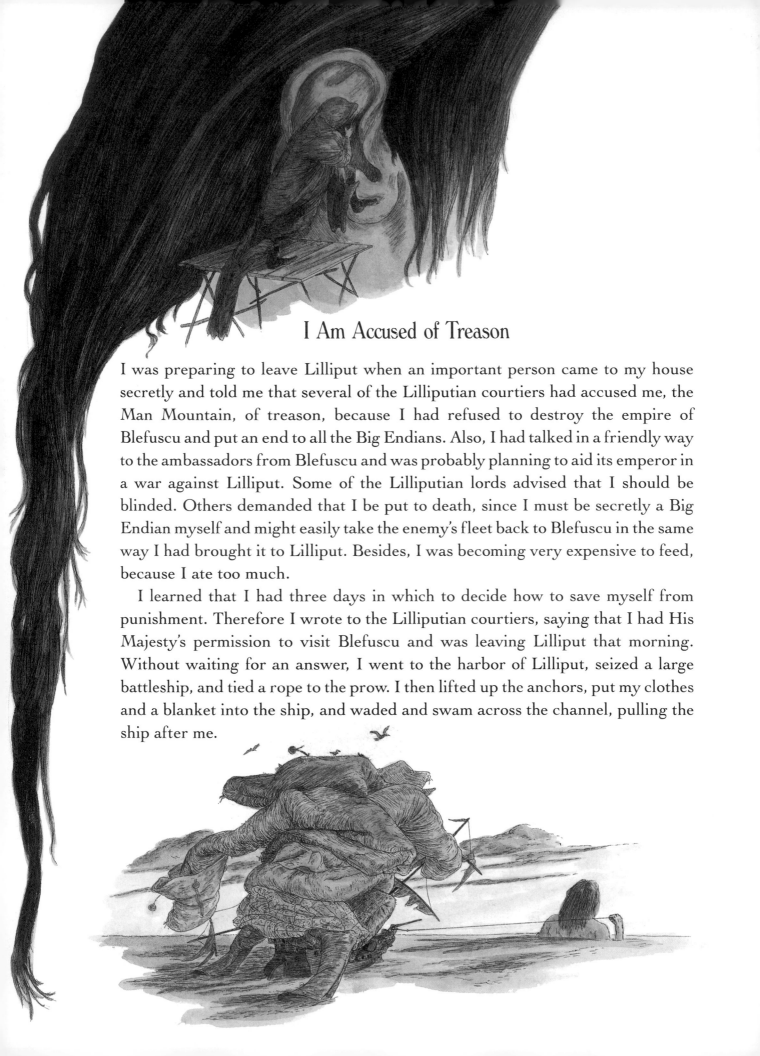

I Am Accused of Treason

I was preparing to leave Lilliput when an important person came to my house secretly and told me that several of the Lilliputian courtiers had accused me, the Man Mountain, of treason, because I had refused to destroy the empire of Blefuscu and put an end to all the Big Endians. Also, I had talked in a friendly way to the ambassadors from Blefuscu and was probably planning to aid its emperor in a war against Lilliput. Some of the Lilliputian lords advised that I should be blinded. Others demanded that I be put to death, since I must be secretly a Big Endian myself and might easily take the enemy's fleet back to Blefuscu in the same way I had brought it to Lilliput. Besides, I was becoming very expensive to feed, because I ate too much.

I learned that I had three days in which to decide how to save myself from punishment. Therefore I wrote to the Lilliputian courtiers, saying that I had His Majesty's permission to visit Blefuscu and was leaving Lilliput that morning. Without waiting for an answer, I went to the harbor of Lilliput, seized a large battleship, and tied a rope to the prow. I then lifted up the anchors, put my clothes and a blanket into the ship, and waded and swam across the channel, pulling the ship after me.

At the royal port of Blefuscu I was shown the way to the capital city, where His Majesty with the royal family and members of the court came out to meet me. They were as small as the people of Lilliput, but they did not seem at all frightened, so I lay on the ground to kiss His Majesty's and the empress's hands. I said to him, "I am honored to meet so mighty a monarch, and I will give any service to Blefuscu that I can offer as a loyal subject of Lilliput."

The emperor of Blefuscu was delighted and entertained me in royal fashion, except that I had to sleep on the ground, wrapped up in my blanket.

A Discovery

Three days later, walking on the northeast coast of Blefuscu, I saw, not far off, something that looked like a boat overturned in the sea. I pulled off my shoes and stockings and waded out, while the tide brought the object nearer. I then saw that it was a real boat, probably blown away from a ship by a tempest.

When I returned to the city with this news, the emperor of Blefuscu agreed to lend me twenty of the tallest ships left after the loss of his fleet. These ships, manned by three thousand seamen, sailed around to meet me where I had discovered the boat. I swam out to it and tied it by a long rope to nine of the ships from Blefuscu, which towed it to the beach. Two thousand men with ropes and pulleys helped me turn it on its bottom. It was not much damaged.

Meanwhile, the emperor of Lilliput had written an angry letter demanding that I return or be declared a traitor who had gone over to the enemy. The emperor of Blefuscu wrote a reply, saying that I had found a huge vessel on the shore and was fitting it up to carry me away, so that both empires would be rid of me.

Souvenirs of the Voyage

In about a month, my boat was ready, stored with cooked meat and bread and drink, provided by the royal kitchens of Blefuscu. I took my leave of the emperor and the royal family, lying flat on the ground to kiss their hands. His Majesty gave me fifty purses of gold coins and a tiny portrait of himself which I put into one of my gloves to keep it safe. I took with me six cows, two bulls, six ewes, and two rams to start new breeds of cattle and sheep in my own country, but the emperor would not permit me to take any of the people.

I set sail on September 24, 1701, at six in the morning. Three days later I spied a sail. As I came up with the ship, my heart leapt within me to see her English colors. I put my cattle and sheep into my coat pockets and with the captain's permission got all my other provisions on board.

The vessel was returning from Japan to England, and among the men, I met an old comrade who asked where I had been. When I told him, he thought I had gone crazy, until I took the cattle and sheep out of my pockets, showed him the emperor's portrait, and gave him a purse of gold from Blefuscu. I promised to give him a cow and a sheep when we reached England.

We arrived on April 13, 1702, safe and sound, except that one of my sheep had been eaten by some of the rats on board ship. The rest of my cattle and sheep were put to grazing in a bowling green where the grass was very fine, and I made a good profit by selling tickets to rich people and others who wanted to see them. I finally sold them for six hundred pounds. Since then, the size of the herds has increased, and I hope that the sheep will provide the finest fleeces to improve the quality of English woolens.

Within two months my family were comfortably settled in a new house, and I could no longer resist traveling again to foreign countries. With tears on both sides, I took leave of my wife and my boy and girl, and went on board the *Adventure*, a ship well named to please me. But I determined that I would never again have anything to do with emperors and courtiers, big or little.

P
96/97
FIC
Hod

Hodges, Margaret.

Gulliver in
Lilliput.

10179

$15.95

P
FIC
Hod

Hodges,
Margaret.

Gulliver in
Lilliput.

$15.95   10179

DATE	BORROWER'S NAME	
OCT 22 '96	Moussavi	4
JAN 28 97	Larson	4
FEB 07		